For robo-son Collin and his wife, Amanda,
to read by the glow of their 1940s X-ray machine. —K. N.

To Dede, skilled mechanic and great dad. —A. B.

STERLING CHILDREN'S BOOKS
New York

An Imprint of Sterling Publishing Co., Inc.
1166 Avenue of the Americas
New York, NY 10036

STERLING CHILDREN'S BOOKS and the distinctive Sterling Children's Books logo
are trademarks of Sterling Publishing Co., Inc.

ISBN 978-1-4549-1064-0

Distributed in Canada by Sterling Publishing Co., Inc.
c/o Canadian Manda Group, 664 Annette Street
Toronto, Ontario, Canada M6S 2C8.
Distributed in the United Kingdom by GMC Distribution Services
Castle Place, 166 High Street, Lewes, East Sussex, England BN7 1XU

For information about custom editions, special sales, and premium and corporate purchases,
please contact Sterling Special Sales at 800-805-5489 or specialsales@sterlingpublishing.com.

Manufactured in China
Lot #:
2 4 6 8 10 9 7 5 3 1
05/16

www.sterlingpublishing.com

The artwork for this book was created digitally.
Designed by Andrea Miller

THE BOT·THAT· SCOTT BUILT

by Kim Norman
illustrated by Agnese Baruzzi

STERLING CHILDREN'S BOOKS
New York

Science Day

This is the bot
the bippity bot,
the rabbit-eared robot,
that Scott built.

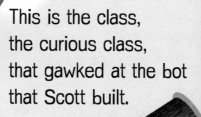

This is the class,
the curious class,
that gawked at the bot
that Scott built.

Science Day

This is the teacher, the talkative teacher, who calmed the class that gawked at the bot that Scott built.

These are the ants,
the angry ants,
that tread on the teacher
in polka-dot pants,
who calmed the class
that gawked at the bot
that Scott built.

These are the plants,
carnivorous plants,
that feasted on flies
and fiery ants,
that tread on the teacher
in polka-dot pants,
who calmed the class
that gawked at the bot
that Scott built.

This is the frog,
the freaky frog,
that leaped from a log
in a bathtub bog,
to gobble the goodies
that piled on plants,
that feasted on flies and fiery ants,
that tread on the teacher
in polka-dot pants,
who calmed the class
that gawked at the bot
that Scott built.

This is the boa,
escaped from its cage,
that draped like a microphone cord
from the stage,
a big-bellied boa
that frightened the frog
(the freaky frog
from the bathtub bog),
that gobbled the goodies
that piled on plants,
that feasted on flies and fiery ants,
that tread on the teacher
in polka-dot pants,
who calmed the class
that gawked at the bot
that Scott built.

Here's the volcano,
the very volcano
that bathed the boa
in vinegar lava,
the big-bellied boa
that frightened the frog

(the freaky frog
from the bathtub bog),
that gobbled the goodies
that piled on plants,
that feasted on flies and
fiery ants,

that tread on the teacher
in polka-dot pants,
who calmed the class
that gawked at the bot
that Scott built.

This is the spark,
the sputtering spark,
that sped overhead
in an awesome arc,
a spark that spit from a Tesla coil
that caused the volcano to bubble and boil . . .

This is the hero,
the handy hero,
who managed the mess
from the very volcano
that bathed the boa
in vinegar lava,
the big-bellied boa
that frightened the frog
(the freaky frog
from the bathtub bog),
that gobbled the goodies
that piled on plants,
that feasted on flies and fiery ants,
that tread on the teacher
in polka-dot pants,
who called for the class . . .

. . . to **CHEER** for the bot that Scott built.